The MAGIC FAN

Written and illustrated by KEITH BAKER

HARCOURT BRACE JOVANOVICH, PUBLISHERS

San Diego   New York   London

Requests for permission to make copies of
any part of the work should be mailed to:
Copyrights and Permissions Department,
Harcourt Brace Jovanovich, Publishers,
Orlando, Florida 32887.

Library of Congress Cataloging-in-Publication Data
Baker, Keith, 1953–
The magic fan/written and illustrated by Keith Baker.
p.   cm.
Summary: Guided by a magic fan, Yoshi builds a boat
to catch the moon, a kite to reach the clouds,
and a bridge that saves the villagers
from a tidal wave.
ISBN 0-15-250750-7
[1. Japan — Fiction. 2. Self-confidence — Fiction.] I. Title.
PZ7.B17427Mag 1989
[E] — dc19   88-18727

First edition

A B C D E

HBJ

The illustrations in this book were done in
Liquitex acrylics on illustration board.

The text type was set in ITC Weidemann Medium
by Thompson Type, San Diego, California.

The display type was set in Elizabeth Roman
by Latent Lettering, New York, New York.

The main title type, based on Elizabeth Roman, was
handlettered by Brenda Walton, Sacramento, California.

Color separations were made by Bright Arts, Ltd., Hong Kong.

Printed and bound by Tien Wah Press, Singapore

Production supervision by Warren Wallerstein and Ginger Boyer

Designed by Michael Farmer

In a village by the sea there lived a boy named Yoshi who loved to build. He built wagons and fences, houses and stairs, tables and walls — everything the people needed, and they were happy listening to the steady sound of Yoshi's tools.

Then one day Yoshi stopped working. "What will you build for us next?" the people asked.

Yoshi could not answer.

That night Yoshi sat by the sea and thought. For hours he listened to the waves and watched the moon.

"There is nothing more I can build for the people. I want to build things I have never built before, things that reach beyond the village, but how can I do that?"

Then Yoshi saw something floating toward him.

"What is this?" he asked as he pulled it from the water. "A fan? In the sea?"

Yoshi opened the fan, and this is what he saw.

On the fan a boat with a golden sail
chased the moon.

"That's it! This fan must be magic —
it has shown me the answer. I will
build a boat that sails across the sea
as fast as the moon sails across the sky."
Yoshi snapped the fan shut and
tucked it securely under his belt.

Through the night and following
day, Yoshi built the wooden hull of
the boat he had seen upon the fan.
From the strongest cloth he cut and
stitched a golden sail.

That evening, the people watched Yoshi push his empty boat out to sea.

"Your boat is gone!" they cried. "Why did you push it away?"

"To catch the moon," said Yoshi. "My boat will sail across the sea tonight."

The people did not understand, for how could a boat ever catch the moon? They returned home to sleep, and all alone Yoshi watched his boat and the moon slip over the horizon together. Then Yoshi looked up at the clouds drifting in to fill the empty sky.

"These clouds must see over the whole world. What could I build to reach so high?"

Yoshi opened the fan, and an answer appeared.

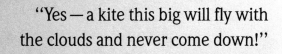

"Yes — a kite this big will fly with the clouds and never come down!"

With long bamboo poles and great sheets of paper, Yoshi built the kite he had seen upon the fan. To finish it he painted wide-open eyes across its enormous face.

At once the kite caught the wind while Yoshi held on with a line of thick rope. The people watched as it rose to the clouds, and there it seemed to be at home.

When the strong wind began to blow the clouds away, Yoshi let the rope slip from his hands.

"Your kite is gone!" the people cried. "Why did you let it go?"

"To look over the world," said Yoshi. "My kite is free like the clouds — nothing will stop it now."

The people shook their heads, for how could a kite look over the world? They returned home to work, leaving Yoshi all alone. As the wind carried his kite and the clouds away, a rainbow stretched across the sky. Yoshi stood and stared.

"What could I build to stretch across the sky like a rainbow?"

Yoshi opened the fan, and an answer appeared.

"A bridge — it will arch from end to end over the village."

For days and days Yoshi worked without stopping. With each cut of the saw and beat of the hammer, Yoshi's bridge grew more like a rainbow. But when Yoshi finally finished and looked down on the village, he saw the shadow of the bridge pass slowly over every house and street.

Far below, the people talked among themselves. "Yoshi's bridge blocks the sun!" they said in anger. "First the boat, then the kite, and now the bridge — we do not need these things. Why has Yoshi built them?"

"The people are right to be angry," thought Yoshi. "My bridge darkens the village. Why did the fan show this to me?"

With tears in his eyes, Yoshi began to cut down his bridge. As he pushed and pulled his saw through the wood, he felt the bridge tremble. Yoshi stopped. Still the bridge trembled; then it shook with a force that seemed to come from the bottom of the sea.

"What shakes the bridge so?" he asked in fear.

Quickly he opened the fan.

Namazu — the earthquake fish! It was awake and angry.

Far out and deep in the sea, Namazu twisted and thrashed wildly. A thundering, monstrous wave — a tsunami — rose out of the water and rushed toward the village.

Yoshi's heart was pounding. He dropped the fan and ran down the bridge.

"Tsunami! Tsunami!" shouted Yoshi, racing up and down the streets of the village.

"I have seen Namazu — a tsunami will soon be here. Follow me!"

Yoshi led the frightened people to the top of his bridge. There they gripped the railing and held tightly to one another.

The tsunami crashed through the village, splintering bamboo fences, crumbling tile stairways, and toppling stone walls. Soon every house was covered by churning waves and spray.

Then, as quickly as it came, the tsunami rolled away. The people could only watch as all of their belongings tumbled far out to sea.

At last the sea was calm again.

"Our village is gone," the people said. "What will we do now?" No one had an answer.

Yoshi searched for the fan, but it, too, was gone, carried away with the tsunami. "Without the magic fan, how will I know what to do?" he asked himself, looking down into the water below. There he saw only his reflection.

Suddenly Yoshi knew the answer, as if the magic fan were open in front of him.

"We can build! Wagons and fences, houses and stairs, tables and walls — everything we need. Together we will rebuild our village. It will be new and beautiful."

"Just like your bridge," the people said. "It has saved us all. The shadow will come and go, but we need the bridge to stand and protect us in our new village, too."

"And when the village is finished," thought Yoshi, "there will be more new things to build — things that reach beyond the village, like bells to talk with thunder, nets to catch the falling stars, and towers to watch for secrets in the sea."

Yoshi could see everything clearly, without the fan. The magic, he had discovered, was his own.